MW01618152

A Brush with Danger

Jacky Yarhi

FELDHEIM

ORIGINALLY PUBLISHED IN HEBREW AS *BEIN KODESH LEMICH'CHOL*

ISBN 978-1-68025-341-2

FELDHEIM PUBLISHERS
POB 43163, JERUSALEM, ISRAEL

208 AIRPORT EXECUTIVE PARK
NANUET, NY 10954
WWW.FELDHEIM.COM

DISTRIBUTED IN EUROPE BY:
LEHMANNS
+44-0-191-430-0333
INFO@LEHMANNS.CO.UK
WWW.LEHMANNS.CO.UK

DISTRIBUTED IN AUSTRALIA BY:
GOLDS WORLD OF JUDAICA
+613 95278775
INFO@GOLDS.COM.AU
WWW.GOLDS.COM.AU

TRANSLATED BY: BROCHA DAVID
COLORIST: SHANI GROSMAN (SHANIGART@GMAIL.COM)

PRINTED IN ISRAEL

ALSO BY JACKY YARHI AND FELDHEIM PUBLISHERS:
SKULLCAPS AND CROSSBONES
WONDERS OF THE BA'AL SHEM TOV
WONDERS OF THE GEDOLIM

Dovid
Yosef
Thomas
The King
Miriam
Saba
Ezra
Uncle Gino
Rav Moshe
Gilliam
The Bishop
The Duke

THE WIND CHANGES DIRECTION...
AND THE DEER PICKS UP THE SCENT OF HUMANS.
I DID IT!

EZRA, WHERE ARE YOU RUNNING?
SABA!
I DID IT!
LOOK AT THIS BEAUTIFUL DEER THAT I DREW!

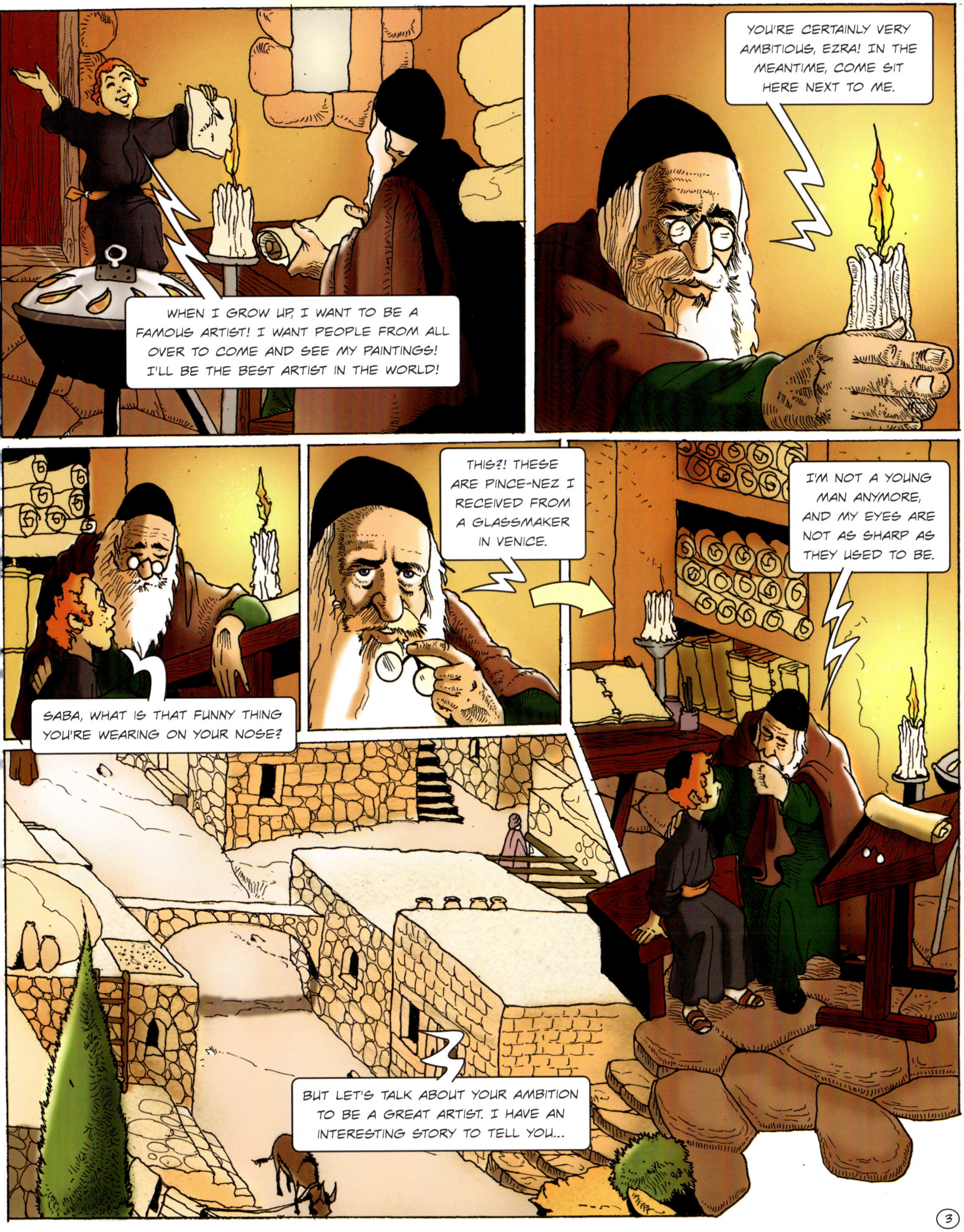

SABA, WHAT IS THAT FUNNY THING YOU'RE WEARING ON YOUR NOSE?

THIS?! THESE ARE PINCE-NEZ I RECEIVED FROM A GLASSMAKER IN VENICE.

I'M NOT A YOUNG MAN ANYMORE, AND MY EYES ARE NOT AS SHARP AS THEY USED TO BE.

BUT LET'S TALK ABOUT YOUR AMBITION TO BE A GREAT ARTIST. I HAVE AN INTERESTING STORY TO TELL YOU...

ACROSS THE SEA, THERE IS A LAND CALLED SPAIN. THE FIRST JEWS TO REACH SPAIN CAME WITH THE ROMAN SOLDIERS WHO CAPTURED THE LAND AND SETTLED THERE.
THE ROMAN EMPIRE SLOWLY GREW WEAKER AND ITS BORDERS WERE INVADED BY BARBARIANS.
THE INVADERS ALLOWED THE JEWS TO LIVE THEIR LIVES IN PEACE AND OBSERVE THEIR RELIGION, BUT THE CHRISTIAN INFLUENCE SPREADING THROUGHOUT EUROPE CAUSED MANY KINGS TO CONVERT TO CHRISTIANITY, AND THE REST OF THE NATION FOLLOWED THEIR EXAMPLE.
UNDER THE INFLUENCE OF THE CHURCH, THE SPANISH MONARCHY, WITH THE ENCOURAGEMENT OF THE CHRISTIAN CLERGY, PLACED VARIOUS RESTRICTIONS ON THE JEWS.

ACROSS THE STRAIT OF GIBRALTAR, ISLAMIC TRIBES FROM THE MAGHREB JOINED FORCES AND SET OUT TO CONQUER THE WORLD.
SPAIN WAS DEFEATED IN BATTLE AFTER BATTLE, UNTIL THE COUNTRY FELL INTO MUSLIM HANDS.
SURPRISINGLY, THE MUSLIMS WERE VERY TOLERANT OF THE JEWS.
JEWS WERE ALLOWED TO OBSERVE THEIR RELIGION IN PEACE, AND IT IS THIS TOLERANCE THAT LED TO WHAT IS KNOWN AS THE GOLDEN AGE OF SPANISH JEWRY.

*POLITICAL AND SPIRITUAL ISLAMIC LEADERS, SUCCESSORS OF MOHAMMED.

**MEMBER OF THE GOVERNMENT, MINISTER.

BUT DURING THE 13TH CENTURY, CHRISTIAN ARMIES BANDED TOGETHER TO WAGE WAR AGAINST THE MUSLIM CONQUERORS OF THE IBERIAN PENINSULA.

ONE AFTER ANOTHER, SPANISH CITIES FELL INTO CHRISTIAN HANDS.

AFTER THE RECONQUEST (THE CHRISTIAN RECAPTURE OF SPAIN FROM ISLAMIC CONTROL), IT SEEMED LIKE THE JEWS WOULD BE ABLE TO CONTINUE LIVING THERE IN PEACE IF THEY SWORE ALLEGIANCE TO THE NEW RULERS.

IS THIS GOOD FOR THE JEWS?
WE DON'T KNOW WHAT THE FUTURE HOLDS FOR US. WE CAN ONLY TRUST IN HASHEM.

THE YEARS PASSED AND CHRISTIAN SPAIN BECAME A POWERFUL EMPIRE, BUILT ON THE RUINS OF ISLAMIC STRUCTURES. HOWEVER, THERE WERE STILL SOME BUILDINGS THAT REMAINED FROM THE ISLAMIC ERA.
WHAT DO YOU SAY, YOSEF? DOESN'T IT SEEM LIKE WE CAN LIVE HERE IN PEACE? THE KING IS PROTECTING US!
GINO, DO YOU REALLY THINK THE KING'S COURT AND THE SPANISH PEOPLE HAVE SUDDENLY CHANGED THEIR STRIPES AND BECOME KIND AND CARING PEOPLE?
BUT EVEN SO, YOU HOLD AN IMPORTANT POSITION IN THE ROYAL COURT...
THE ONLY REASON I'M THERE IS BECAUSE THE KING IS CONVINCED THAT JEWS ARE TALENTED PEOPLE WHEN IT COMES TO MONEY MATTERS!

IN FACT, I'M ON MY WAY TO THE PALACE RIGHT NOW.
HAVE A GOOD DAY, MY DEAR BROTHER-IN-LAW.
YOUR ROYAL HIGHNESS! ROME HAS EXPRESSED DISPLEASURE AT THE CHOICES YOU HAVE MADE.
SURELY YOU ARE REFERRING TO THE FACT THAT I HIRE JEWISH ADVISORS!
THEY ARE OUR ENEMIES, YOUR HIGHNESS!
THERE ARE CRUSADERS WHO ARE TRAVELING ACROSS THE WORLD TO FIGHT HOLY WARS, WHILE OUR JOB HERE IS TO CLEANSE OUR OWN EMPIRE OF...
ENOUGH! I DON'T WANT TO HEAR ANOTHER WORD!

JUST YOU WAIT...
WE'LL SOON SEE
WHAT'S IN STORE
FOR YOU...

HERE YOU ARE! HAVE YOU FOUND A SOLUTION TO THE PROBLEM?

AT THE SAME TIME IN THE QUEEN'S QUARTERS...
HELLO, FATHER THOMAS! DO YOU HAVE ANY NEWS FOR US?

YES, YOUR MAJESTY! WE ARE A NAVAL EMPIRE AND IT WOULD BE WISE OF US TO TAKE ADVANTAGE OF THAT.

WE MUST TAKE ACTION IMMEDIATELY.

WE SHOULD SEND OUR FLEETS TO SEA TO SEARCH FOR NEW MARKETS.

BUT I LIKE YOUR IDEA. LET ME THINK ABOUT IT. YOU CAN GO NOW...

AT THAT MOMENT...

I NEED HIM IN ORDER FOR MY PLAN TO SUCCEED...

*THE CHURCH CLAIMED THAT THE EARTH WAS FLAT AND THUS SHIPS COULD NOT SAIL TOO FAR IN THE OPEN SEAS.

*ONE OF THE CHRISTIAN CHURCH'S MAIN ACCUSATIONS AGAINST THE JEWS.

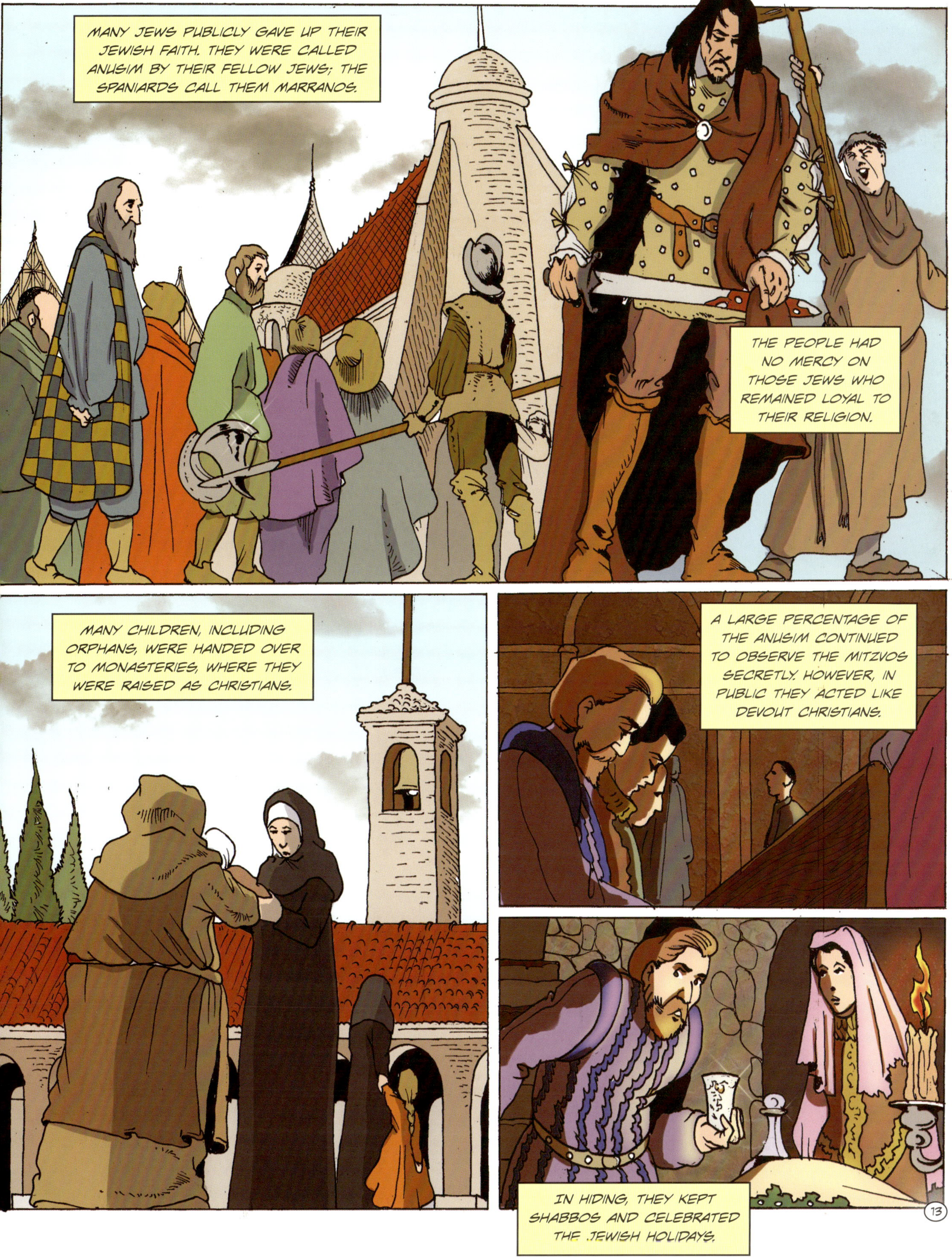

MANY JEWS PUBLICLY GAVE UP THEIR JEWISH FAITH. THEY WERE CALLED ANUSIM BY THEIR FELLOW JEWS; THE SPANIARDS CALL THEM MARRANOS.

THE PEOPLE HAD NO MERCY ON THOSE JEWS WHO REMAINED LOYAL TO THEIR RELIGION.

LEADING A DOUBLE LIFE LIKE THIS WAS FRAUGHT WITH DANGER. ANY JEW WHO DID NOT ACCEPT CHRISTIANITY WAS SENTENCED TO DEATH.
FATHER, WHY ARE WE GOING TO THIS PLACE INSTEAD OF THE SYNAGOGUE?

QUIET, MY SON! YOU MUST FORGET ALL ABOUT YOUR OLD LIFE.

TEMPTED BY THE REWARD OFFERED BY THE CHURCH TO THOSE WHO INFORMED ON SECRET JEWS, THE SPANIARDS PERSECUTED THE ANUSIM AND ACCUSED THEM OF HERESY.

THE CHRISTIAN CLERGY TAUGHT THE SERVANTS OF THE ANUSIM EXACTLY WHAT TO LOOK FOR.
COME HERE A MOMENT, MY DAUGHTER...

ARE YOU THE ONE WHO WORKS FOR THE RODRIGUEZ FAMILY?

YES, FATHER.
ON SATURDAY, DOES THE FAMILY DO ANYTHING STRANGE? DO THEY LIGHT CANDLES ON FRIDAY NIGHT?

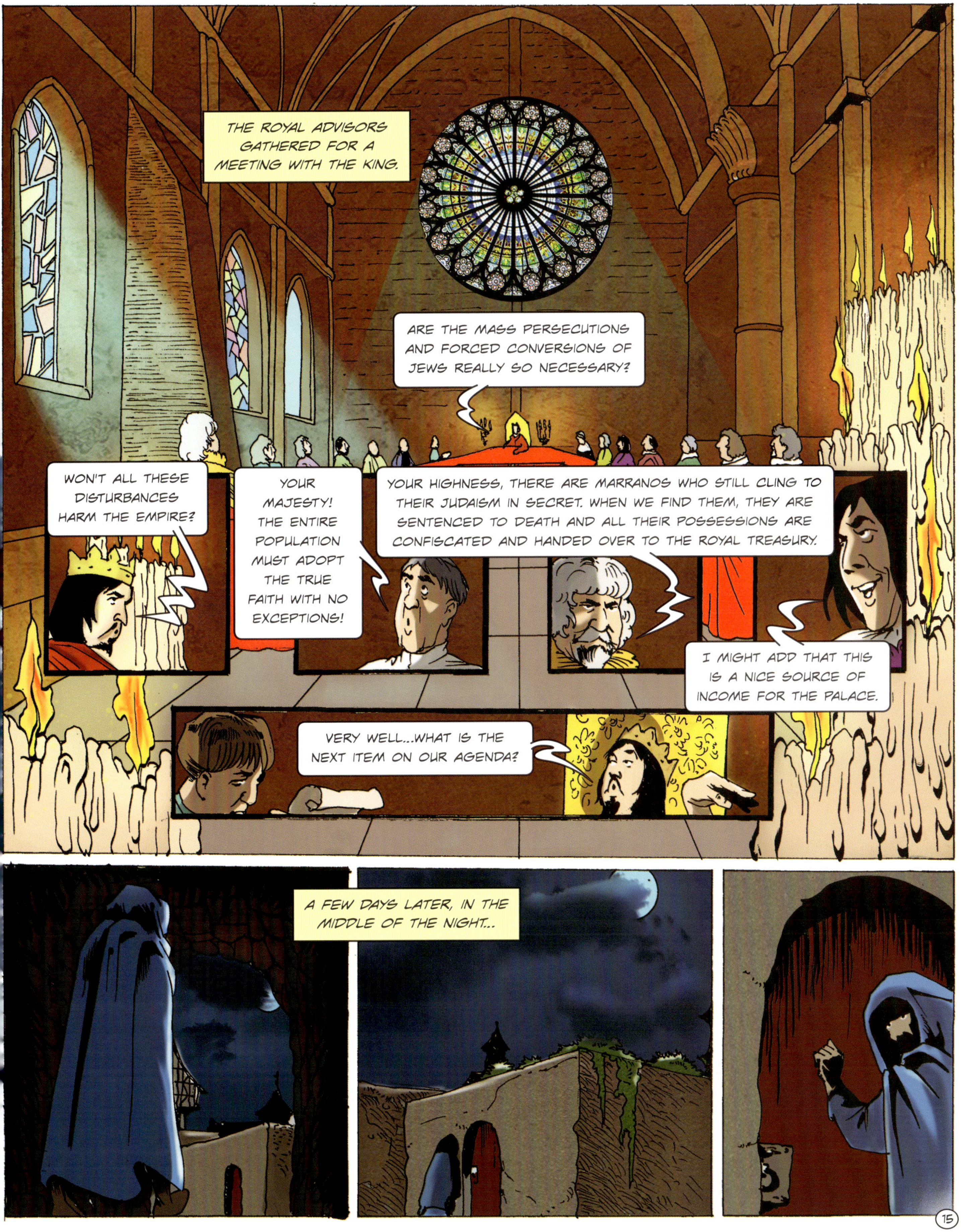

THE ROYAL ADVISORS GATHERED FOR A MEETING WITH THE KING.

ARE THE MASS PERSECUTIONS AND FORCED CONVERSIONS OF JEWS REALLY SO NECESSARY?

WON'T ALL THESE DISTURBANCES HARM THE EMPIRE?

YOUR MAJESTY! THE ENTIRE POPULATION MUST ADOPT THE TRUE FAITH WITH NO EXCEPTIONS!

YOUR HIGHNESS, THERE ARE MARRANOS WHO STILL CLING TO THEIR JUDAISM IN SECRET. WHEN WE FIND THEM, THEY ARE SENTENCED TO DEATH AND ALL THEIR POSSESSIONS ARE CONFISCATED AND HANDED OVER TO THE ROYAL TREASURY.

I MIGHT ADD THAT THIS IS A NICE SOURCE OF INCOME FOR THE PALACE.

VERY WELL...WHAT IS THE NEXT ITEM ON OUR AGENDA?

*ACCORDING TO LEGEND, CHRISTOPHER COLUMBUS RECEIVED FUNDING FROM JEWS WHO HOPED TO FIND A SAFE HAVEN WHERE THEY COULD LIVE OPENLY AS JEWS.

IN THE KING'S PALACE...
YOSEF, DO YOU KNOW WHY I BROUGHT YOU HERE, TO THE TOP OF THIS TURRET?
FROM HERE, YOU CAN SEE THE ENTIRE CITY AND THE LAND SPREAD OUT AT OUR FEET. WE CONQUERED THIS LAND FROM THE MUSLIM INFIDELS.
BUT THERE ARE SOME SPANIARDS WHO BELIEVE THAT THE CONQUEST IS NOT COMPLETE AS LONG AS THE JEWS LIVING HERE DENY CHRISTIANITY.
MY WIFE, THE QUEEN, BELIEVES EVERYTHING HER PRIEST TELLS HER. SHE IN TURN INFLUENCES THE OPINIONS OF THE MEMBERS OF MY ROYAL COURT.
DO YOU MEAN TO SAY THAT ALL OF SPAIN'S JEWS ARE IN DANGER?
CONVERT, AND I WILL APPOINT YOU TO THE HIGHEST POSITION IN THE EMPIRE, SECOND ONLY TO ME.
YOU'RE STUBBORN, AREN'T YOU? I THOUGHT YOU WOULD BE...

MOTHER, UNCLE GINO IS ON HIS WAY HERE!

TIMES ARE GETTING HARDER. SINCE OUR FRIEND MENASHE WAS BURNED AT THE STAKE, I HAVEN'T HAD A MOMENT'S PEACE OF MIND.
YOUR DEVOTION IS AN INSPIRATION TO ALL OF US. ARE MY SON'S TEFILLIN READY?
INDEED THEY ARE, AND I HAVE SOMETHING ELSE FOR YOU AS WELL...

I WOULD LIKE TO GIVE YOU A SCROLL THAT IS VERY PRECIOUS TO ME.

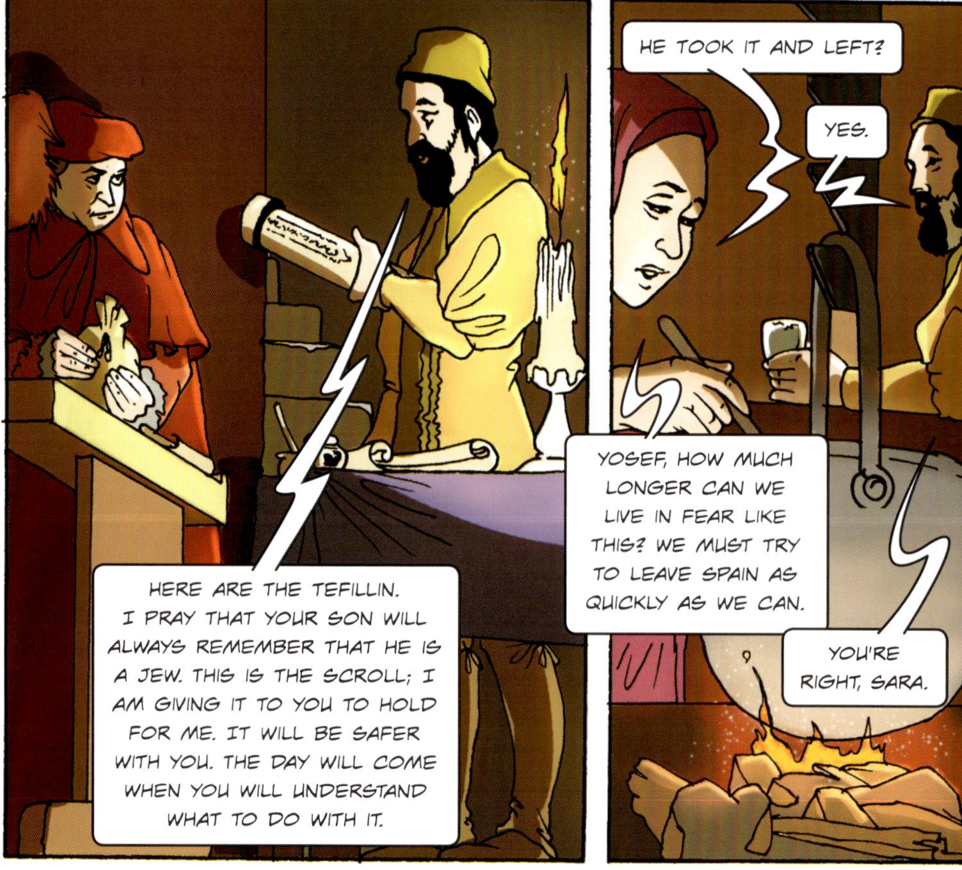
HERE ARE THE TEFILLIN. I PRAY THAT YOUR SON WILL ALWAYS REMEMBER THAT HE IS A JEW. THIS IS THE SCROLL; I AM GIVING IT TO YOU TO HOLD FOR ME. IT WILL BE SAFER WITH YOU. THE DAY WILL COME WHEN YOU WILL UNDERSTAND WHAT TO DO WITH IT.
HE TOOK IT AND LEFT?
YES.
YOSEF, HOW MUCH LONGER CAN WE LIVE IN FEAR LIKE THIS? WE MUST TRY TO LEAVE SPAIN AS QUICKLY AS WE CAN.
YOU'RE RIGHT, SARA.

FATHER, DID YOU SEE HOW NICE MY HANDWRITING IS?
YES, DOVID, AND I'M NOT SURPRISED. BEAUTIFUL SCRIPT RUNS IN THE ABUTRANI FAMILY.
EVERYONE KNOWS YOU AS A HIGH-RANKING FINANCIAL OFFICER IN THE GOVERNMENT. BUT, FATHER, I KNOW THAT YOU REALLY PUT MOST OF YOUR TIME AND EFFORT INTO YOUR SECRET ACTIVITIES IN THE CELLAR. YOU WRITE TEFILLIN, MEZUZAHS, AND EVEN *SIFREI TORAH* AND MEGILLAHS. THAT'S DANGEROUS WORK, FATHER!
DOVID, MY SON, THE JOB OF SOFER HAS BEEN PASSED DOWN THROUGH OUR FAMILY FOR GENERATIONS.
HASHEM HAS BLESSED US WITH A RARE TALENT—AN EXQUISITE, SPARKLING HANDWRITING THAT CAN BE USED FOR *TASHMISHEI KEDUSHAH*. IT IS A GIFT FROM HEAVEN AND WE MUST USE IT FOR THE SAKE OF HASHEM.
YOU TOO HAVE INHERITED THIS GIFT. YOU KNOW HOW TO GENTLY GRASP THE QUILL AND PRODUCE LOVELY SCRIPT.
I PROMISE YOU, FATHER, THAT ONE DAY I WILL CONTINUE OUR FAMILY'S LEGACY...
OUR ORDERS ARE TO CHAIN HIM AND BRING HIM IN FOR INTERROGATION, AT ANY PRICE!

DEEP IN THE INQUISITION'S TORTURE CHAMBER, YOSEF THE SCRIBE WAS CRUELLY TORTURED BUT REFUSED TO REVEAL THE NAMES OF THE ANUSIM WHOM HE PROVIDED WITH TASHMISHEI KEDUSHAH. WITHIN A SHORT TIME, YOSEF DIED FROM HIS WOUNDS.
FATHER IS A TRUE HERO, AND NOW HE IS WATCHING US FROM GAN EDEN. I AM CERTAIN THAT WHAT HE WANTS FROM US MOST OF ALL IS TO ESCAPE FROM ACCURSED SPAIN AS QUICKLY AS WE CAN.
BUT HOW IS THAT POSSIBLE, MOTHER? THERE ARE SPIES AND INFORMERS LURKING IN EVERY CORNER...
THEY WON'T SUSPECT ME OF PLANNING ANYTHING; AFTER ALL, I'M JUST A SERVANT. I'LL TAKE CARE OF ALL THE NECESSARY ARRANGEMENTS.
THANK YOU, MIRIAM. I DON'T KNOW HOW I WOULD HAVE SURVIVED THESE DIFFICULT TIMES WITHOUT YOUR HELP AND ENCOURAGEMENT.
I HEAR A KNOCK ON THE DOOR. I WONDER WHO IT COULD BE. SINCE FATHER WAS TAKEN BY THE INQUISITION, NO ONE WANTS TO COME TO OUR HOUSE ANYMORE.
WH...WH... WHAT DO YOU WANT?
HELLO, DOVID. IT'S UNCLE GINO. DON'T YOU RECOGNIZE ME?!

PLEASE BELIEVE ME, I AM A LOYAL JEW. I WAS A CLOSE FRIEND OF YOUR FATHER AND I AM SO HAPPY THAT MY SON RECEIVED TEFILLIN WRITTEN BY HIM.
THEN...THEN WHY ARE YOU WEARING THAT CLOAK, THE SORT WORN BY OUR OPPRESSORS?

WHEN I WAS CAUGHT BY THE INQUISITION ABOUT A YEAR AGO, I WAS TORTURED MERCILESSLY. OUTWARDLY, I SWORE ALLEGIANCE TO THE CHURCH AND I WAS FORCED TO WORK FOR THE INQUISITION ITSELF.
DID YOU MEET MY FATHER AGAIN BEFORE HE DIED?

I DID INDEED.

I AM AFRAID I WILL NEVER SEE MY WIFE AND SON AGAIN. DO YOU REMEMBER THE PRECIOUS SCROLL THAT I ENTRUSTED TO YOU? WHEN I DIE, I ASK YOU TO PLEASE GO TO MY HOUSE AND GIVE THE SCROLL TO MY FAMILY. TELL THEM THAT I WANT THEM TO HURRY AND ESCAPE FROM SPAIN TO A PLACE WHERE THEY CAN LIVE A FULL JEWISH LIFE.

DID MY FATHER SAY ANYTHING ELSE? PLEASE TRY TO REMEMBER! HIS EVERY WORD IS SO PRECIOUS TO ME...
YES, YOUR FATHER SAID THAT HE WROTE THIS SCROLL ESPECIALLY FOR YOU. YOU ARE TO GUARD IT CAREFULLY, AND WHEN YOU GROW UP YOU WILL CONTINUE THE FAMILY CHAIN AND BECOME A SCRIBE YOURSELF.

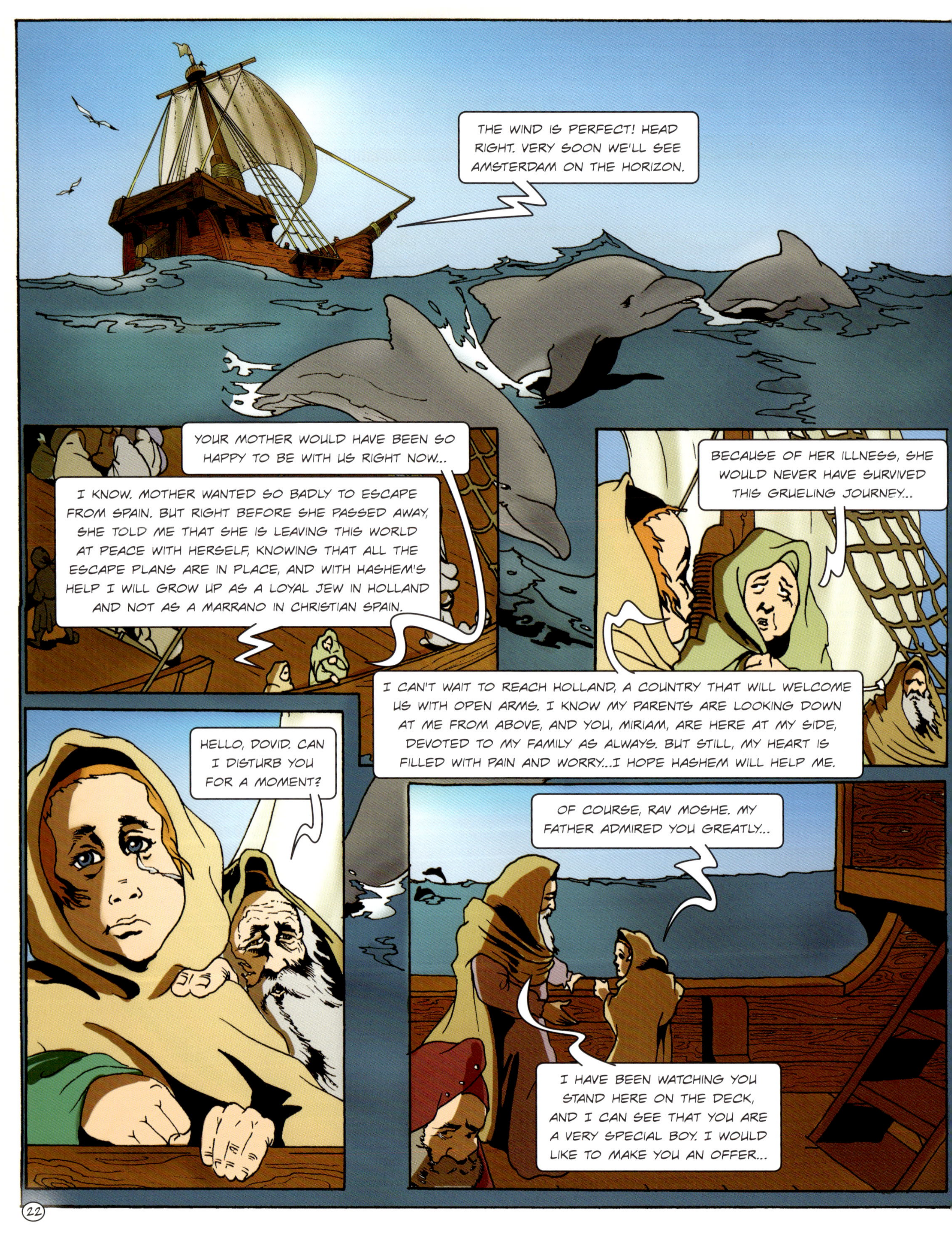
THE WIND IS PERFECT! HEAD RIGHT. VERY SOON WE'LL SEE AMSTERDAM ON THE HORIZON.
YOUR MOTHER WOULD HAVE BEEN SO HAPPY TO BE WITH US RIGHT NOW...
I KNOW. MOTHER WANTED SO BADLY TO ESCAPE FROM SPAIN. BUT RIGHT BEFORE SHE PASSED AWAY, SHE TOLD ME THAT SHE IS LEAVING THIS WORLD AT PEACE WITH HERSELF, KNOWING THAT ALL THE ESCAPE PLANS ARE IN PLACE, AND WITH HASHEM'S HELP I WILL GROW UP AS A LOYAL JEW IN HOLLAND AND NOT AS A MARRANO IN CHRISTIAN SPAIN.
BECAUSE OF HER ILLNESS, SHE WOULD NEVER HAVE SURVIVED THIS GRUELING JOURNEY...
I CAN'T WAIT TO REACH HOLLAND, A COUNTRY THAT WILL WELCOME US WITH OPEN ARMS. I KNOW MY PARENTS ARE LOOKING DOWN AT ME FROM ABOVE, AND YOU, MIRIAM, ARE HERE AT MY SIDE, DEVOTED TO MY FAMILY AS ALWAYS. BUT STILL, MY HEART IS FILLED WITH PAIN AND WORRY...I HOPE HASHEM WILL HELP ME.
HELLO, DOVID. CAN I DISTURB YOU FOR A MOMENT?
OF COURSE, RAV MOSHE. MY FATHER ADMIRED YOU GREATLY...
I HAVE BEEN WATCHING YOU STAND HERE ON THE DECK, AND I CAN SEE THAT YOU ARE A VERY SPECIAL BOY. I WOULD LIKE TO MAKE YOU AN OFFER...

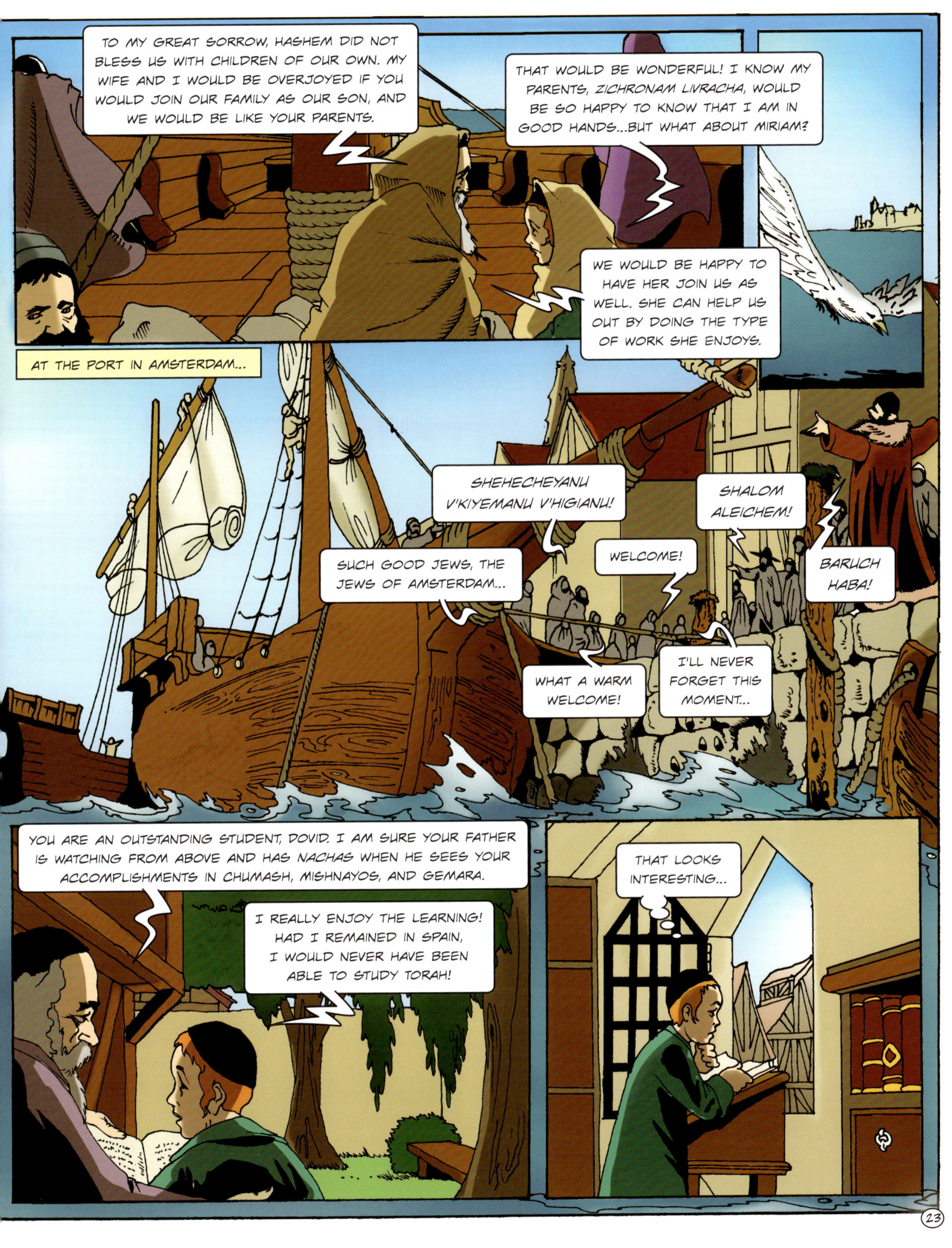

TO MY GREAT SORROW, HASHEM DID NOT BLESS US WITH CHILDREN OF OUR OWN. MY WIFE AND I WOULD BE OVERJOYED IF YOU WOULD JOIN OUR FAMILY AS OUR SON, AND WE WOULD BE LIKE YOUR PARENTS.
THAT WOULD BE WONDERFUL! I KNOW MY PARENTS, ZICHRONAM LIVRACHA, WOULD BE SO HAPPY TO KNOW THAT I AM IN GOOD HANDS...BUT WHAT ABOUT MIRIAM?
WE WOULD BE HAPPY TO HAVE HER JOIN US AS WELL. SHE CAN HELP US OUT BY DOING THE TYPE OF WORK SHE ENJOYS.
AT THE PORT IN AMSTERDAM...
SHEHECHEYANU V'KIYEMANU V'HIGIANU!
SHALOM ALEICHEM!
SUCH GOOD JEWS, THE JEWS OF AMSTERDAM...
WELCOME!
BARUCH HABA!
WHAT A WARM WELCOME!
I'LL NEVER FORGET THIS MOMENT...
YOU ARE AN OUTSTANDING STUDENT, DOVID. I AM SURE YOUR FATHER IS WATCHING FROM ABOVE AND HAS NACHAS WHEN HE SEES YOUR ACCOMPLISHMENTS IN CHUMASH, MISHNAYOS, AND GEMARA.
I REALLY ENJOY THE LEARNING! HAD I REMAINED IN SPAIN, I WOULD NEVER HAVE BEEN ABLE TO STUDY TORAH!
THAT LOOKS INTERESTING...

WHAT AN AMAZING ARTIST! INCREDIBLE!

I SEE YOU ARE INTERESTED IN MY ARTWORK. WHAT DO YOU THINK OF THIS PAINTING?
IT'S BEAUTIFUL! DO YOU MIND IF I WATCH YOU WORK?

NOT AT ALL. MY NAME IS GILLIAM VAN DER RAN. WHAT'S YOUR NAME?
DOVID.

IT'S A LITTLE HARD FOR ME TO COPY LETTERING IN A FOREIGN LANGUAGE...
CAN I TRY?

YOU HAVE REAL TALENT. PERHAPS... PERHAPS YOU'D LIKE TO BE MY ASSISTANT?

YOU MAY NOT REALIZE IT, BUT YOU HAVE RARE TALENT.
I CAN TELL JUST BY THE WAY YOU HOLD THE PAINTBRUSH.
YOUR ASSISTANT? WH...WHAT DO YOU MEAN?
I NEED TO THINK ABOUT YOUR OFFER.
I'LL WAIT FOR YOU HERE TOMORROW EVENING, AND I HOPE TO RECEIVE A POSITIVE REPLY.
I'LL EXPLAIN ONCE AGAIN, DOVID. IT IS SO IMPORTANT FOR YOU TO SPEND THE PRECIOUS YEARS OF YOUR YOUTH LEARNING TORAH.
YOUR FATHER, WHO IS WATCHING OVER YOU FROM GAN EDEN, IS EXPECTING YOU TO DO JUST THAT. REMEMBER THE PROMISE YOU MADE TO HIM, THAT YOU WOULD CONTINUE HIS LEGACY AND GROW UP TO BE A SOFER!
I WILL DO AS YOU SAY, RAV MOSHE. THANK YOU FOR GUIDING ME AND SHOWING ME THE WAY.
I HOPE YOUR ANSWER WILL MAKE ME HAPPY.
I THANK YOU FOR YOUR GENEROUS OFFER, BUT I HAVE DECIDED NOT TO ACCEPT RIGHT NOW.
IS THAT SO?! ALL RIGHT, THEN. I BELIEVE WE WILL MEET AGAIN...
RAV MOSHE WAS RIGHT. LEARNING TORAH REALLY IS SWEETER THAN HONEY. THE SUGYA I'M LEARNING NOW IS FASCINATING! I WONDER IF MY TEACHER OR RAV MOSHE WILL FIND AN ANSWER TO MY QUESTION.

I AM ALMOST CERTAIN THAT THIS IS WHERE THAT TALENTED JEWISH BOY LIVES.

GILLIAM THE ARTIST! WHAT A SURPRISE... HOW DID YOU KNOW WHERE I LIVE?
I GUESSED. I CAME TO SAY GOOD-BYE. TOMORROW I SET SAIL ON A VERY EXCITING JOURNEY. I HAVE BEEN INVITED TO DECORATE ONE OF THE MOST BEAUTIFUL PALACES IN ITALY.

WELL THEN, WE WISH YOU A SAFE TRIP AND ALL THE BEST!
JUST ONE MOMENT; WITH YOUR PERMISSION, I WOULD LIKE TO HAVE A WORD WITH THE BOY. I WANT TO MAKE HIM A ONCE-IN-A-LIFETIME OFFER. IF HE ACCOMPANIES ME ON MY JOURNEY, I WILL HAVE A VERY GIFTED ASSISTANT...

...AND HE WILL HAVE AN AMAZING OPPORTUNITY TO DEVELOP HIS TALENTS AND ACCOMPLISH GREAT THINGS IN THE FIELD OF ART.

THE SHIP SETS SAIL TOMORROW AFTERNOON. YOU HAVE UNTIL THEN TO THINK ABOUT IT, DOVID.

I NEED YOUR ADVICE, MIRIAM; YOU ARE WISE AND YOU HAVE LIFE EXPERIENCE. YOU HEARD GILLIAM'S WORDS AND ALSO WHAT RAV MOSHE SAID.
HELP ME DECIDE IF I SHOULD FOLLOW MY HEART TO ITALY OR FOLLOW MY HEAD, WHICH TELLS ME TO STAY HERE.
I CAN'T DECIDE FOR YOU. BUT WHETHER YOU STAY OR GO, I WILL REMAIN RIGHT AT YOUR SIDE, JUST LIKE I PROMISED YOUR MOTHER BEFORE SHE DIED.

I KNEW HE WOULD COME IN THE END...
WONDERFUL!
WE WILL WAIT FOR YOU EVERY SINGLE DAY. WE HOPE YOU'LL BE BACK SOON, STRONG IN YOUR FAITH AND LOYAL TO THE TORAH.
YOU SEE, MIRIAM, WE'VE BEEN TRAVELING FOR SOME TIME NOW AND I CAN SEE THAT I MADE THE RIGHT DECISION.
I HAVE TIME TO LEARN MISHNAH AND GEMARA HERE JUST LIKE I DID IN AMSTERDAM. THANKS TO YOUR SUPERVISION IN THE KITCHEN, I HAVE KOSHER MEALS, AND I AM LEARNING A LOT ABOUT ART FROM GILLIAM.
TIME WILL TELL IF IT WAS REALLY A WISE DECISION. IN THE MEANTIME, I PRAY THAT HASHEM WILL WATCH OVER YOU.
GET READY, DOVID! THE "ITALIAN BOOT" IS BEFORE US. WELCOME TO ITALY.
THEY'VE PREPARED A NICE WELCOME FOR US, BUT SOMETHING TELLS ME THAT WE HAVE TO BE VERY CAREFUL...

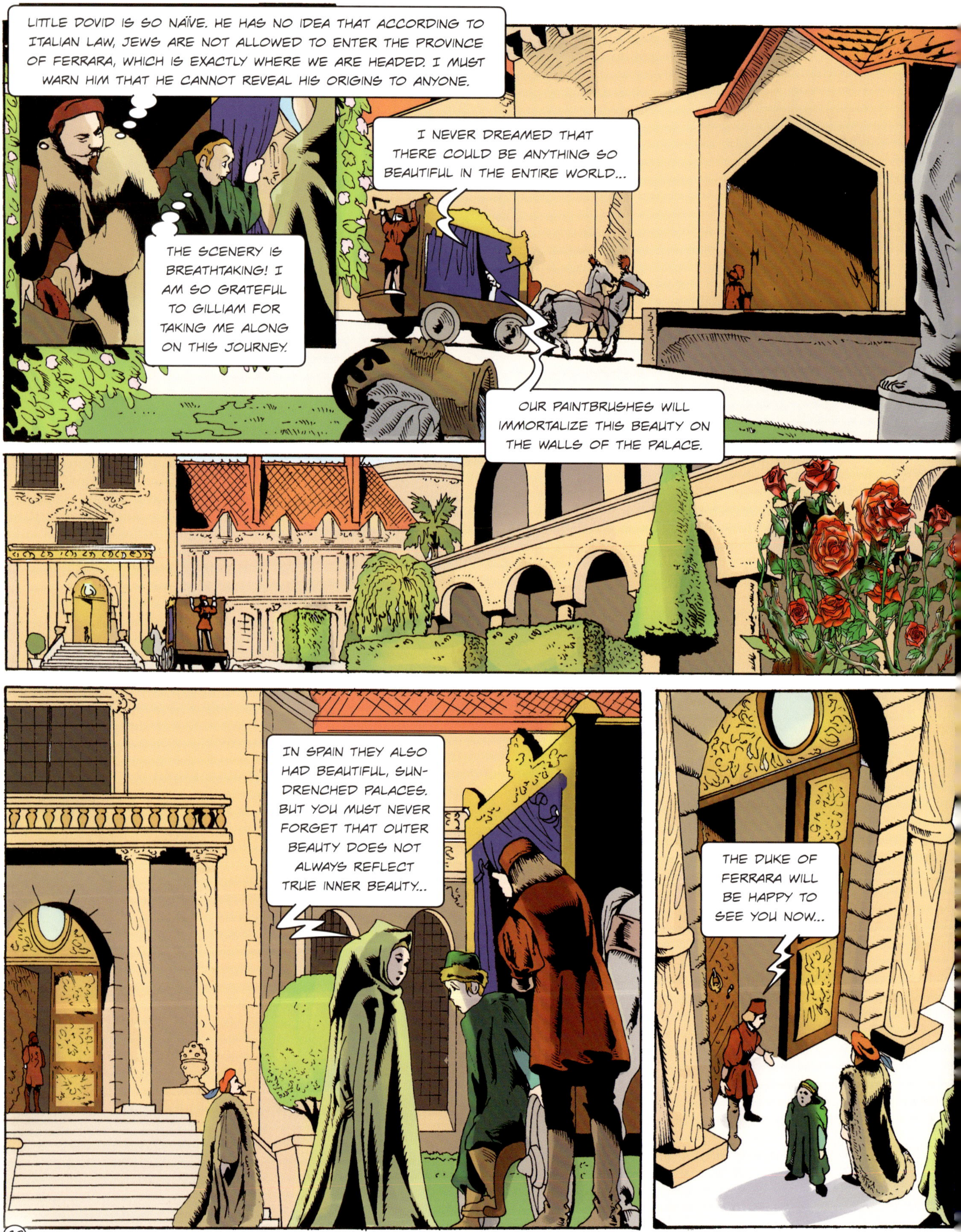

LITTLE DOVID IS SO NAÏVE. HE HAS NO IDEA THAT ACCORDING TO ITALIAN LAW, JEWS ARE NOT ALLOWED TO ENTER THE PROVINCE OF FERRARA, WHICH IS EXACTLY WHERE WE ARE HEADED. I MUST WARN HIM THAT HE CANNOT REVEAL HIS ORIGINS TO ANYONE.

THE SCENERY IS BREATHTAKING! I AM SO GRATEFUL TO GILLIAM FOR TAKING ME ALONG ON THIS JOURNEY.

I NEVER DREAMED THAT THERE COULD BE ANYTHING SO BEAUTIFUL IN THE ENTIRE WORLD...

OUR PAINTBRUSHES WILL IMMORTALIZE THIS BEAUTY ON THE WALLS OF THE PALACE.

THERE'S SOMETHING IMPORTANT I NEED TO TELL YOU. YOU MUST NOT REVEAL TO A SOUL IN THE PALACE THAT YOU ARE JEWISH.
WH...WHAT?! NOW YOU'RE TELLING ME THAT MY JEWISHNESS IS A PROBLEM HERE?

WELL, IT'S TOO LATE TO TURN BACK NOW. I'LL JUST HAVE TO BE VERY CAREFUL.

YOUR ASSIGNMENT IS TO PAINT THE CEILING AND THE WALLS OF THE MAIN HALLS WITH STUNNING DESIGNS. YOU SEE, NO ONE IN ITALY LOVES AND APPRECIATES BEAUTY AS MUCH AS I DO. I HOPE I MAKE MYSELF CLEAR. THIS IS TO BE THE MOST EXQUISITE PALACE IN ALL OF ITALY.

ON THIS WALL I WANT A PORTRAIT OF MYSELF RIDING A HORSE.

AND HERE, I WANT MY LIKENESS SURROUNDED BY THE BEAUTIFUL LANDSCAPES OF FERRARA.

I AM VERY PLEASED.
THE DUKE MAY HAVE DELUSIONS OF GRANDEUR, BUT WE WILL BOTH MAKE A LOT OF MONEY AS A RESULT.

MY MASTER HAS PROVIDED LODGINGS FOR YOU RIGHT HERE IN THE PALACE.
WE HAVE TAKEN YOUR REQUEST INTO CONSIDERATION AND ARRANGED A SPACIOUS AND COMFORTABLE WING FOR YOU, WITH A LOVELY VIEW.

WE HAVE ALSO TRIED TO TAKE YOUR REQUESTS INTO CONSIDERATIO YOUNG LAD. YOU'LL SLEEP IN THE GARDEN ROOMS SOME DISTANC FROM THE PALACE. OF COURSE, WE WILL BE HAPPY TO HOST YOU THE PALACE ITSELF SHOULD YOU CHANGE YOUR MIND.

THESE ROOMS ARE FOR YOU AND YOUR GOVERNESS.

YOUR GOVERNESS EXPLAINED TO ME THAT FOR HEALTH REASONS, YOU REQUIRE A SPECIAL DIET AND YOU WILL NOT BE TAKING YOUR MEALS IN THE PALACE.
WE HAVE SET UP A KITCHEN FOR YOU AND WE WILL SEND YOU FOODSTUFFS AS WELL.

YOU ARE DOING A WONDERFUL JOB, MY BOY. I DON'T KNOW HOW I WOULD HAVE HANDLED SUCH A BIG JOB WITHOUT YOU.

I WONDER HOW THOSE TWO ARTISTS I BROUGHT FROM HOLLAND ARE COMING ALONG WITH THEIR WORK.

EXCELLENT WORK!
EXCELLENT!

INDEED, OUR WORK IS THE RESULT OF MUCH TIME AND EFFORT.
CERTAINLY. AND TALENT TOO.

OF COURSE. IT WAS BECAUSE OF MY TALENT THAT YOU HIRED ME, WAS IT NOT?
YES, INDEED. BUT I KNEW NOTHING OF THE RARE TALENT OF THIS VERY SPECIAL BOY. I NEVER HEARD OF HIM BEFORE...

YOUNG MAN, DO YOU LIKE TO DRAW?
YES, SIR, VERY MUCH.
I AM SURE YOU WILL GO FAR.

GOOD MORNING TO YOU, DILIGENT ARTISTS!
GOOD MORNING TO YOU TOO, SIR!

YOU'VE DRAWN AN INCREDIBLE BIRD, MY BOY. YOU HAVE GOLDEN HANDS. YOUR PAINTING IS UTTERLY CAPTIVATING.
EH...HEM... AND WHAT ABOUT THE FLOWER THAT I'VE DRAWN, SIR? DO YOU NOT THINK IT IS LOVELY?!

DUKE RUDOLPHO COMPLIMENTED THE BOY'S WORK AGAIN! WHY DID I EVER BRING HIM HERE? HE'LL STEAL MY FAME AND FORTUNE.

I MUST FIND A WAY TO DEAL WITH THIS!

BARUCH HASHEM, THE DUKE IS PLEASED WITH MY WORK. IT'S TOO BAD THAT GILLIAM HAS BECOME SO SHORT-TEMPERED LATELY. I DON'T UNDERSTAND WHAT'S BOTHERING HIM.

I HAVE GREAT NEWS FOR YOU, MY FRIEND. NEXT MONTH, I WILL HOST AN EXCLUSIVE PARTY IN THE PALACE. THE GUESTS OF HONOR WILL BE NONE OTHER THAN OUR TWO DISTINGUISHED ARTISTS FROM HOLLAND!

IS THAT SO?! THEN I MUST WARN YOU, SIR, THAT IT MIGHT BE PROBLEMATIC FOR YOU TO INVITE THE YOUNG BOY...

I DON'T UNDERSTAND. WHY SHOULD THERE BE ANY PROBLEM WITH INVITING THE BOY TO A PARTY?
BECAUSE THERE ARE A FEW THINGS ABOUT HIM THAT YOU DON'T KNOW. THE BOY IS A JEW. ARE YOU PLANNING TO SERVE KOSHER FOOD AT THIS PARTY OF YOURS?

A JEW?!

DUKE RUDOLPHO HAS SUMMONED YOU TO AN URGENT MEETING IN EXACTLY HALF AN HOUR.

MIRIAM, I'M WORRIED ABOUT THIS UNEXPECTED MEETING. TELL ME WHAT I SHOULD DO.
GO, AND MAY HASHEM PUT THE RIGHT WORDS IN YOUR MOUTH.

HOW EMBARRASSING IT WILL BE IF ANYONE FINDS OUT THAT MY PALACE WAS DECORATED BY A JEW! ALL OF MY ARISTOCRATIC FRIENDS WILL MOCK ME TO NO END.

YOU HID THE FACT THAT YOU ARE A JEW! ACCORDING TO LAW, JEWS ARE NOT ALLOWED TO ENTER FERRARA.

A JEW WILL NOT DECORATE MY PALACE! IS THAT ABSOLUTELY CLEAR? AS A JEW, YOU MAY NOT REMAIN HERE.
I UNDERSTAND. IF SO, THEN I MUST CHOOSE...

YOU HAVE THREE DAYS TO DECIDE IF YOU WANT TO BE A CHRISTIAN ARTIST OR A BANISHED JEW!

I'VE DECIDED TO LEAVE FERRARA TOMORROW AT DAWN. I CERTAINLY DON'T NEED THREE DAYS TO THINK ABOUT IT!
I AM PROUD OF YOU, DOVID. YOU HAVE PASSED A DIFFICULT TEST.

GILLIAM, I'M SORRY TO TELL YOU THAT SOMEHOW THE DUKE DISCOVERED THAT I AM A JEW. THANK YOU FOR THE OPPORTUNITY TO WORK AT YOUR SIDE, BUT TOMORROW MORNING I'M LEAVING...
WHY?! DID THE DUKE FORCE YOU TO LEAVE?

HE DEMANDED THAT I CONVERT. OF COURSE I WOULD NEVER CONSIDER SUCH A THING. THEREFORE, I HAVE NO CHOICE BUT TO LEAVE.

I JUST WANTED THE DUKE TO DISLIKE THE BOY. I DIDN'T THINK HE WOULD BANISH HIM! WHAT WILL I DO NOW? I'LL NEVER BE ABLE TO FINISH THE WORK ON MY OWN!

I CANNOT ALLOW YOU TO LEAVE JUST NOW. I NEED YOUR HELP TO COMPLETE THE WORK. AND I WILL MISS YOUR PLEASANT COMPANY AS WELL.

STRANGE. LATELY, IT DOESN'T SEEM LIKE HE FINDS MY COMPANY SO "PLEASANT."

PLEASE, DON'T GO YET. I WILL TRY TO SPEAK TO THE DUKE.

THE POOR BOY THINKS I'M ON MY WAY TO THE DUKE. HE HAS NO IDEA THAT I'M HEADING TO THE BISHOP OF FERRARA...

DO YOU UNDERSTAND? THE DUKE IS SIMPLY ALLOWING THE JEW TO LEAVE THE COUNTRY SCOT-FREE!

I WILL NOT ALLOW THAT TO HAPPEN!

IF THE HONORABLE BISHOP FORCES DOVID TO CONVERT, HE WILL STAY HERE AND HELP ME PAINT THE PALACE.

G-D OF AVRAHAM, YITZCHAK, AND YAAKOV, PLEASE WATCH OVER DOVID, SON OF THE HOLY MARTYRS YOSEF AND SARA.

YOU SNEAKED INTO THE CHRISTIAN PROVINCE OF FERRARA, CONCEALED YOUR JEWISHNESS, LIED, CHEATED, AND DECEIVED US. ACCORDING TO THE LAW, I CAN PUT YOU IN PRISON FOR THE REST OF YOUR LIFE.

IT'S A PITY. WHY SHOULD A YOUNG, TALENTED BOY LIKE YOU ROT IN JAIL FOR SO MANY YEARS? I CAN FREE YOU EASILY, THOUGH. ALL YOU HAVE TO DO IS CONVERT.
NEVER! I WILL NOT BETRAY MY G-D OR MY PEOPLE.

I AM A JEW AND I WILL ALWAYS BE A JEW!

TO PRISON! TAKE HIM AND HIS GOVERNESS. LOCK THEM UP IN TWO SEPARATE CELLS IN THE DARK, DAMP DUNGEON.

THANK YOU, RIBBONO SHEL OLAM, FOR GIVING DOVID THE COURAGE AND STRENGTH TO STAND UP TO OUR OPPRESSORS. PLEASE, HASHEM, HELP HIM IN THE MERIT OF HIS HOLY PARENTS...

YOU CAN CRY, WAIL, AND YELL ALL YOU WANT. NO ONE WILL EVER HEAR YOU THROUGH THESE THICK STONE WALLS.
MY G-D WILL HEAR ME. I WILL CRY TO HIM AND MY PRAYERS WILL GO STRAIGHT UP TO HIS HEAVENLY THRONE.

RIBBONO SHEL OLAM, I KNOW I SHOULD HAVE LISTENED TO RAV MOSHE AND STAYED IN AMSTERDAM. I FORGOT THAT MY TALENT IS A GIFT FROM HEAVEN, A GIFT YOU GAVE ME SO THAT I COULD CONTINUE THE FAMILY CHAIN AND BECOME A SOFER.
BECAUSE OF ME AND MY FOOLISHNESS, POOR MIRIAM IS SUFFERING TERRIBLY.

THE DUKE WOULD IKE TO KNOW WHAT THE CONDITIONS RE LIKE IN ALL THE JAILS IN FERRARA. HE APPOINTED ME O VISIT EVERY JAIL O MAKE SURE THAT HE PRISONERS ARE OT SUFFERING FROM BHUMAN CONDITIONS.
GO RIGHT AHEAD. WE HAVE NOTHING TO HIDE.

ALL RIGHT, THE CONDITIONS HERE CERTAINLY SEEM REASONABLE.

THAT'S STRANGE. I'M ALMOST CERTAIN THAT HE DROPPED ME THIS NOTE ON PURPOSE.

Now I know where you are. Be ready tonight at exactly midnight. Do whatever you are told.

FOLLOW ME.

BUT WHAT ABOUT MIRIAM?

OH, BARUCH HASHEM, MIRIAM IS HERE TOO. PLEASE TELL ME, WHO ARE YOU? WHO SENT YOU TO SAVE US?
THE DUKE SENT ME. HE IS ACTUALLY QUITE FOND OF YOU AND IT SEEMED TO HIM A SHAME FOR YOU TO SIT IN JAIL JUST BECAUSE YOU ARE A JEW.
DO YOU MEAN THAT THE DUKE WAS NOT THE ONE WHO INFORMED ON ME TO THE BISHOP? IF SO, THEN WHO WAS IT?
IT WAS YOUR FRIEND GILLIAM, OF COURSE. HE'S THE ONE WHO TOLD THE DUKE THAT YOU ARE JEWISH IN THE FIRST PLACE, AND HE IS THE ONE WHO RAN TO THE BISHOP TO TATTLE ON YOU.
RAV MOSHE NEVER LIKED HIM AND NEITHER DID I...
I DON'T UNDERSTAND...I TRUSTED HIM, AND I FOLLOWED HIM ALL THE WAY TO ITALY...
ON ORDERS FROM DUKE RUDOLPHO, ALL YOUR POSSESSIONS ARE ON BOARD THE SHIP, WHICH WILL TAKE YOU TO SAFETY IN TURKEY.
THANK YOU, AND PLEASE GIVE THE DUKE MY HEARTFELT THANKS AS WELL.
HOW BLIND I WAS! HOW COULD I HAVE ABANDONED WHAT I HAD, TORAH STUDY AND LOVING ADOPTIVE PARENTS, IN EXCHANGE FOR THE SLIPPERY PROMISES OF A GENTILE ARTIST?
HASHEM, IN HIS KINDNESS, IS GIVING YOU A SECOND CHANCE TO CHOOSE THE RIGHT PATH.

AMONG THE ITEMS RETURNED TO HIM BY THE DUKE OF FERRARA, DOVID FINDS A SILVER CASE.

INSIDE, RESTS A SCROLL WRITTEN IN HIS FATHER'S HAND.

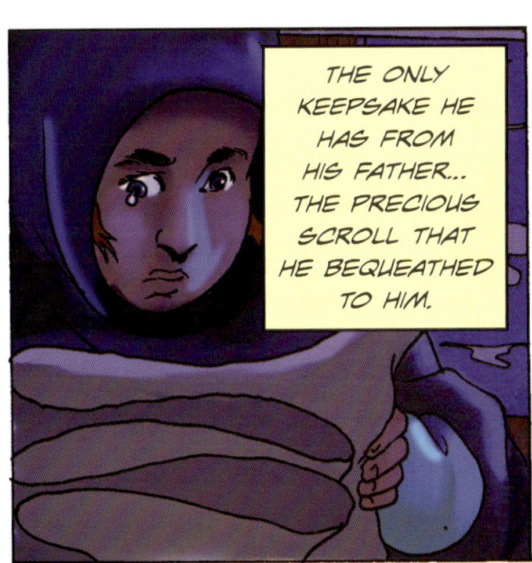
THE ONLY KEEPSAKE HE HAS FROM HIS FATHER... THE PRECIOUS SCROLL THAT HE BEQUEATHED TO HIM.

THE DAYS PASS SLOWLY UNTIL...

FINALLY...
LAND!
LAND AHOY!

WE'LL FEEL SAFE HERE IN THIS LAND.
MAY HASHEM HEAR YOUR WORDS...
!

THERE THEY ARE!

I MUST SPEAK TO THEM!

SHALOM ALEICHEM!
GREETINGS.

YOU ARE JEWS, ARE YOU NOT?
WE ARE INDEED...

YOU HAVE NOTHING TO FEAR. WE ARE THE LEADERS OF THE JEWISH COMMUNITY AND OUR REPRESENTATIVE IS ALWAYS ON HAND TO WELCOME NEWLY ARRIVED REFUGEES.

WE WILL TAKE GOOD CARE OF YOU.

SURE ENOUGH, THE MEMBERS OF THE TURKISH JEWISH COMMUNITY FIND LODGINGS FOR DOVID AND MIRIAM AND PROVIDE THEM WITH SUPPORT AND ASSISTANCE.
IT IS MY HONOR TO HOST YOU IN MY HUMBLE HOME.

MY HOME IS YOUR HOME.

AS DOVID GROWS UP, HE BECOMES A SOFER, AND HIS SCRIPT IS AS BEAUTIFUL AS HIS LATE FATHER'S.

TIME PASSES AND DOVID FEELS A BURNING DESIRE TO RETURN TO THE LAND OF OUR FOREFATHERS, ERETZ YISRAEL. MIRIAM, WHO IS AN ELDERLY WOMAN BY THEN, REMAINS IN TURKEY.
DOVID ARRIVES IN ERETZ YISRAEL, MARRIES, AND ESTABLISHES A FAMILY.

COME WITH ME.

SABA, IS THIS A TREASURE?
EVEN BETTER THAN THAT...

MUCH BETTER, EZRA...
THE SCROLL...

SABA, YOU ARE DOVID! I SHOULD HAVE GUESSED!
YES...AND DOVID HAD A SON...
...AND THAT SON IS YOUR FATHER.

EVERY SCRIBE IN OUR FAMILY RECORDS HIS LIFE STORY ON THIS SCROLL. I'VE WRITTEN THE STORY I JUST TOLD YOU, AS MY FATHER DID BEFORE ME. IF YOU FOLLOW IN OUR FOOTSTEPS, ONE DAY YOU WILL ALSO WRITE YOUR STORY HERE.

COME, LET'S TAKE A LITTLE WALK. I WANT TO EXPLAIN SOMETHING TO YOU.

EZRA, WHAT DO YOU SEE ALL AROUND YOU?

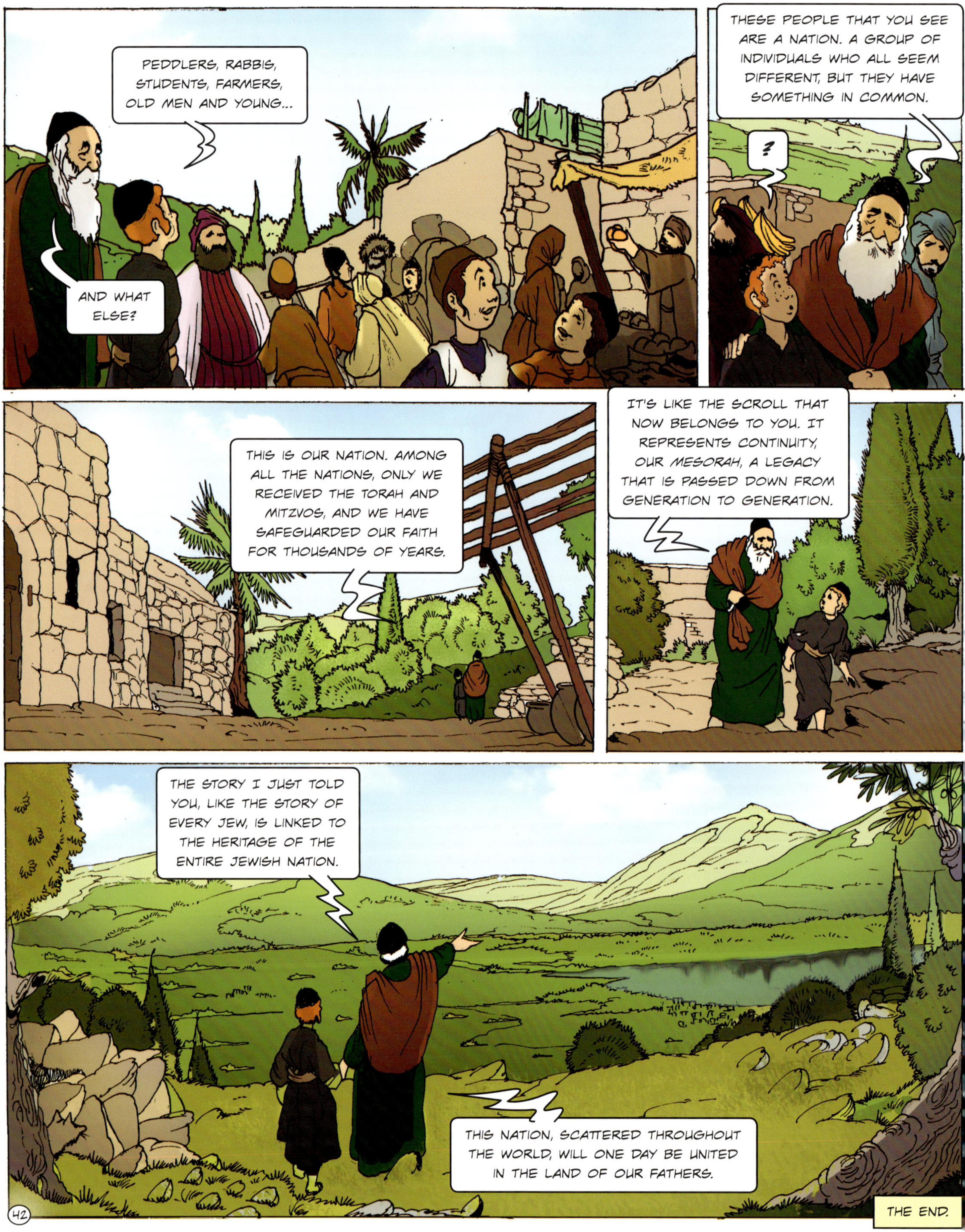

THE STORY I JUST TOLD YOU, LIKE THE STORY OF EVERY JEW, IS LINKED TO THE HERITAGE OF THE ENTIRE JEWISH NATION.

THIS NATION, SCATTERED THROUGHOUT THE WORLD, WILL ONE DAY BE UNITED IN THE LAND OF OUR FATHERS.

THE END.

North Sea
Atlantic Ocean
Amsterdam
Ferrara
Barcelona

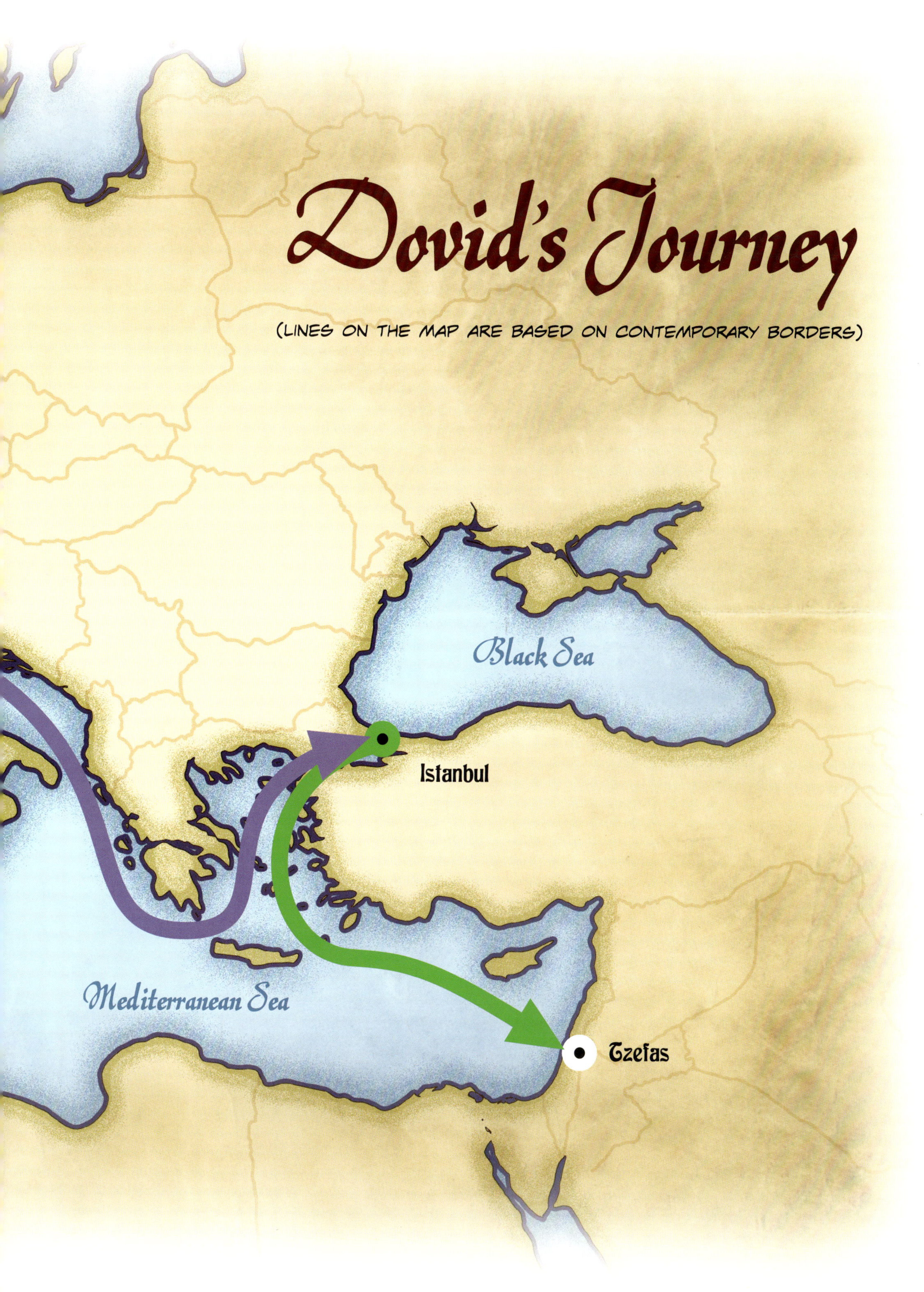

Dovid's Journey
(LINES ON THE MAP ARE BASED ON CONTEMPORARY BORDERS)
Black Sea
Istanbul
Mediterranean Sea
Tzefas